D0591138

Bod's Present

Michael and Joanne Cole

EGMONT

EGMONT

We bring stories to life

Original hardback edition first published in Great Britain 1965 by Methuen & Co. Ltd.
This edition first published in Great Britain 2015 by Egmont UK Limited,
The Yellow Building, 1 Nicholas Road, London W11 4AN
www.egmont.co.uk

Endpaper and cover design by Lo Cole

ISBN 978 1 4052 7754 9

A CIP catalogue record for this title is available from the British Library.

Here is Bod, walking in the snow. It's Christmas Eve, and he's taking a Christmas present to his Aunt Flo. "I had better hurry," says Bod. "It's snowing hard."

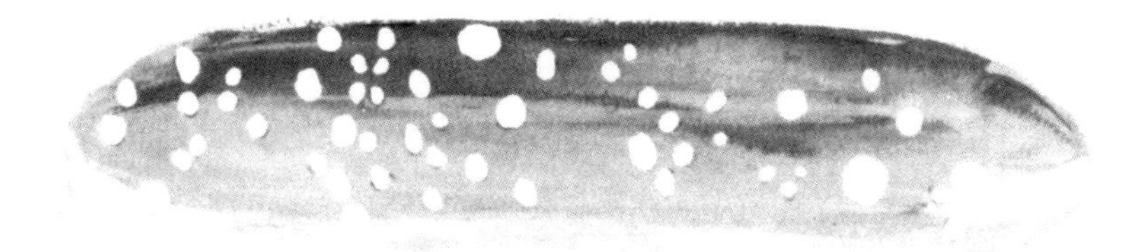

He has only gone a little way when he sees somebody ahead of him, trudging through the snow. It's P.C. Copper. Bod catches up with him. "Hello," he says.

"Hello, hello," says P.C. Copper.
"Where are you off to?"
"I'm taking a present to Aunt Flo," says Bod.
"So am I!" says P.C. Copper.

They go on together. The snow is getting deeper all the time. Then ahead of them they see a figure struggling through the snow. It's Frank the postman. They catch up with him.

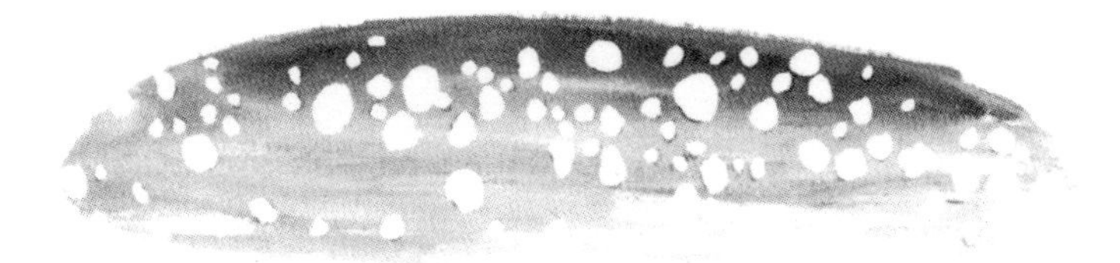

"Hello, hello," says P.C. Copper.
"Where are you going?"
"I'm taking a present to Aunt Flo," says Frank.
"So are we!" says P.C. Copper.

They struggle on together through the snowstorm. The snow comes up to their waists, and they can hardly move. After a while they see somebody else trying to get through the snow.

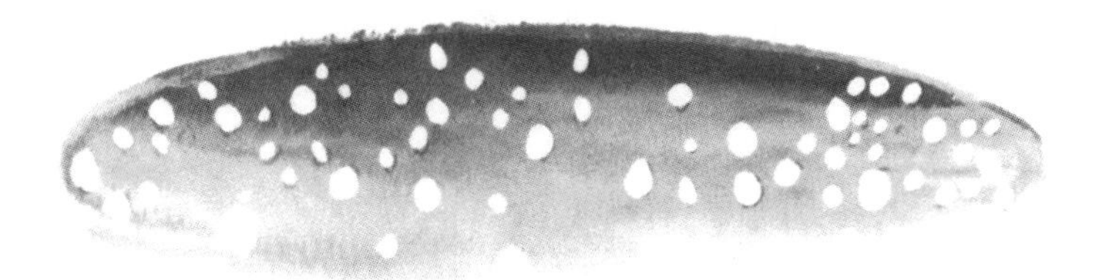

It's Farmer Barleymow. They catch him up.
"Hello," says Frank. "Going to Aunt Flo's?"
"I'm trying to," says Barleymow.
"So are we!" says Frank.

They try to go on together, but the snow is too deep. It comes up to their necks. They're stuck. And the flakes are whirling down and settling faster than ever.

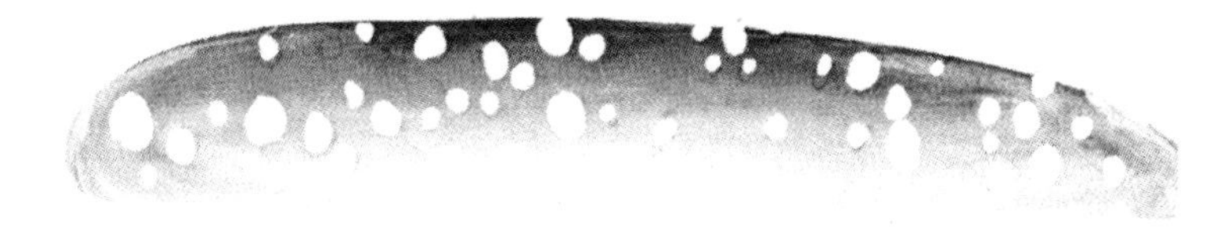

"Cold, isn't it?" says Barleymow.

"Yes," says Frank.

"Yes," says P.C. Copper.

Bod is too cold to answer.

Night falls. The snow comes up over their heads. Midnight chimes in the distance. Everything is very still and quiet. Then there is a jingle of bells, and out of the night rides Father Christmas on his sleigh.

"Whoa there! Whoa!" he cries to his reindeer, when he sees the four parcels in the snow. "Someone must have dropped these presents for Aunt Flo," he says, reading the labels. "I had better take them to her."

He goes to pick the first parcel up, but he can't move it. He gives a tremendous tug. It moves a little. He gives an even bigger tug, and up it comes with Bod on the end.

"Hello," says Bod.

Then Bod helps Father Christmas pull the others out of the snow.

"Jump in, and I'll give you a lift," says Father Christmas.

"Thank you," says Bod.

They all jump into the sleigh, and off they go like the wind.

"Getting you out of the snow has made me a bit late," says Father Christmas. "Would you help me deliver some presents on the way?"

"We'd love to," says Bod.
Father Christmas gives them each a sack of presents, and they all go down chimneys, and put the presents into the stockings the children have hung up by their beds.

When they have delivered the presents, Father Christmas takes them to Aunt Flo's house. They say goodbye to him and watch him ride away into the dawn. Then they go down Aunt Flo's chimney.

She is already up and making herself a cup of tea.
"Happy Christmas!" says Bod.
Aunt Flo jumps, and pours tea all over the floor.
"Oh, what a fright you gave me!" she says.

Then Bod gives his present to Aunt Flo.
She opens it. It's a hat.

"It's gorgeous," says Aunt Flo, putting it on.

"Thank you, Bod. How kind of you."

"Happy Christmas," says P.C. Copper.
And he gives Aunt Flo his present.
She opens it. It's another hat.

"It's gorgeous," says Aunt Flo, putting it on over the first hat. "What a kind copper you are!"

Then Farmer Barleymow gives his present.
"Guess what it is," he says.
"I've no idea," says Aunt Flo.
She opens it. It's another hat.

"What a gorgeous hat!" says Aunt Flo, putting it on over the other two. "How good of you, Barleymow, to find time from all your ploughing and sowing to go and buy me a hat!"

"Happy Christmas!" says Frank, giving Aunt Flo his present. "It's another hat for you, I'm afraid."

"What a hatty Christmas I'm having!" says Aunt Flo, putting the hat on over the other three.

"Now it's my turn," says Aunt Flo.
"A very happy Christmas to you all."

She hands four presents to Frank.
"Pass them along, will you?" she says.

Aunt Flo has given them all handkerchiefs. "Thank you so much," says Bod. "These handkerchiefs will come in very nosy. I mean these nosekerchiefs will come in very handy . . ."

In fact what he means is that Aunt Flo couldn't have given a more useful present, for Bod and his friends have all caught colds from their night in the snow.

But it was worth catching a cold, thinks Bod, to meet Father Christmas, and to see Aunt Flo in all those hats. Didn't she look stunning?
Happy Christmas, Bod.
"Happy . . . Happy . . . Happy . . .

ATISHOO-MAS!" says Bod.